POLONIUM'S TREASURE

Written by
Quentin Flynn

Illustrated by
Brent Putze

HORWITZ
MARTIN
EDUCATION

Contents

Chapter 1
Two Strangers Arrive

Two shiny new vehicles moved carefully along the cobblestone street, one after the other, before turning into the village square. Everyone sitting at the tables lining the piazza looked up from their coffee, and eyed the motor vehicles. Who were these strangers?

Unlike many other tiny Italian villages, Poloni was not used to tourists visiting through the summer. A new arrival was a big event in Poloni — two arrivals was positively remarkable.

"People from the city," whispered Antonio, pointing. His sister, Maria, quickly looked up from their game of marbles.

"They must be lost," she said, as she returned her concentration to her next shot. "No-one ever comes to Poloni deliberately!" And with a flick of her thumb, she knocked one of Antonio's prize glass marbles out of the chalk circle.

"I win!" she announced loudly. "I win!"

As usual, Antonio ignored her. He was trying to read the lettering along the side of the first car.

"Institute of Archaeology," he read out loud.

"What's 'archaeology'?" asked Maria.

"It's digging up old things. You know, Roman stuff," replied Antonio.

"Maybe they've come to visit Mrs Rivoli's sweet shop," said Maria cheekily. "Half the lollies in there are so old even the Romans wouldn't buy them."

"Excuse me, children!" sang a high-pitched, squeaky voice. A large man, with a thin weedy moustache, waddled right through the chalk circle, accidentally kicking the marbles left and right.

"Hey!" protested Maria. "Watch where you're going!"

But the man just ignored her protests and carried on walking towards the spot where the vehicles had been parked. He was waving his hands in the air, and loudly clearing his throat.

"Shh!" said Antonio. "That's Mr Gruffio, the mayor. Be quiet, otherwise he'll probably make a law banning marbles in the square."

Maria knew full well that the man was Mr Gruffio. In the year since he had come to Poloni, he had already banned kite flying, bicycle riding, and skateboards anywhere in Poloni's square. Right now he was occupying the number one spot on Maria's P.S.D. list of 'People She Disliked'.

"I don't care if he *is* the mayor. He's rude and mean," she grumbled. "As if Poloni wasn't boring enough, he's stopped everyone from having any fun at all. Just because he's a lazy, boring old bully, he thinks we should be the same."

"Welcome!" came Gruffio's loud booming voice from across the square. He held out his flabby hand to a woman who was climbing out of the first vehicle. "You must be Miss Limoni?"

"Professor Limoni, actually," smiled the woman, taking Gruffio's hand and shaking it vigorously. Gruffio looked exhausted by the effort. He took a large, dirty handkerchief out of his pocket and mopped his sweaty forehead.

"Of course, forgive me, Professor Limoni," he said, smiling weakly.

"And this is Professor Roberts," continued the woman, introducing the man who had just stepped out of the second vehicle. "From America."

"America," breathed Gruffio, who seemed to think that the very word was dripping with money. "Welcome, welcome! I hope you will enjoy your stay in our humble little village."

The American smiled politely and looked at Gruffio who was now sweeping his arms around pointing out the features of the village.

The village square was lined with little metal tables and chairs where curious villagers sat. There was a small church to one side of the square, and a straggling row of stone houses leading out of the village. A cafe, a bakery, and Mrs Rivoli's sweet shop seemed to be the only businesses in the little township.

Beyond the village lay row upon row of grapevines and behind them, in the dark fertile soil, grew hundreds of twisted old olive trees.

Overshadowing the whole scene was Mount Pyros, a sleepy giant blue-green volcano, shimmering in the summer heat.

"Very pleasant," replied the American. "I'm sure we will enjoy our stay — even if we *are* working."

Gruffio bowed and then he waved his arm across the square, searching for a comfortable chair.

"Please, let's sit down and you can tell me all about your work. I understand you are looking for the fabled Roman town of Polonium."

Maria groaned as she watched the mayor steering the man and woman straight towards the table next to where they were playing marbles.

"Typical!" she murmured. She knew what was going to happen next. Mayor Gruffio would start acting as if he owned the place.

"Of course, we all know the rumours about Polonium — about the fabled great treasure that it hides," Gruffio began. "Oh, excuse me!"

The major peered at Antonio and Maria as if they had just magically appeared from nowhere. He flapped his hands at them as though he was chasing away an annoying blowfly.

"Shoo!" he said. "Peasants," he explained to his embarrassed guests. "Ignore them."

"Hello," said Professor Limoni to the children, trying to make up for the mayor's bad behaviour. Maria shot her an angry glance, gathered up the last of the marbles, and stalked out of the square.

Antonio followed her, relieved that Maria hadn't chosen to use her latest rude word on Gruffio. That probably would have ended up with *them* being banned from the square, as well as being banned from playing marbles.

"How dare he!" cried Maria furiously, as she stomped up the gentle slope and out of town. "We've got just as much right as anyone to play in the square!"

Antonio and Maria trudged up the hill towards the small farm where they lived. Their father, Armenio, was out in the field, rebuilding a small stone wall, but Maria ignored him and marched straight into the house, slamming the door behind her. Armenio walked slowly down the sloping field towards his son.

"What's wrong with her?" he asked. Antonio shrugged.

"Gruffio," he replied. His father grinned.

"That man knows how to upset even the youngest residents of Poloni," he said. "Banned marbles now, has he?"

"Not yet," said Antonio glumly. "But it won't be long." He brightened up as he remembered the new arrivals. Like all the villagers, his father would be interested to hear about them.

"Two professors!" he said excitedly, as he told his father about the visitors. "And one of them is an American. How about that?"

"How about that, indeed," laughed Armenio. "One day people will realise that all this talk about Polonium is just a fairy tale. All we have here are

grapes and olives — and that's all we've had for
hundreds of years."

Armenio was right. For hundreds of years there
had been nothing else in this spot but a small
village and its crops. What he didn't know,
however, was that, deep beneath his feet, lay a
secret that had lain in silence for much, much
longer. Thousands of years, in fact.

Chapter 2

Some New Friends

The next morning, Antonio reluctantly followed his sister down the path to the village square.

"It's my square too, and I'm going to play marbles there," she had declared forcefully after breakfast. "Are you coming, or are you scared of old goofy Gruffio?"

Faced with a challenge like that, Antonio could hardly refuse. He gathered up his marbles, put them in his pocket, and ran after his sister.

But, when they arrived, the square was deserted. It was still too early for most of the villagers to gather and discuss their news over coffee at one of the shiny tables. Feeling confident, Maria drew a huge circle in the middle of the square with a piece of chalk.

"There," she said. "Not even Gruffio can be stupid enough to miss that!" She spaced out her marbles inside the circle, and grinned at Antonio.

"Go on, you first," she continued. Antonio looked around nervously, and took out a marble from his pocket. It was duller than the rest, but it had a curious mix of colours deep below its glassy surface. It was Antonio's favourite marble.

Aiming carefully, he flicked it at Maria's tombola but it bounced off with a loud click and rolled right out of the circle.

"Ha!" said Maria. "My turn!" She aimed an aggie at Antonio's marble and with a quick flick whacked that out of the circle too, laughing as it rolled to a halt.

Suddenly, a shadow loomed over the circle, and both children jerked their heads up. A figure had silently crept up to where they were playing, and now stood staring from above.

"Hello," said the woman who they had seen arrive in the motor vehicle the day before. "I'm sorry we spoiled your game yesterday."

"That's OK," said Antonio quickly, before Maria could get a word in. "It's just marbles," he shrugged. His sister glared at him.

"I'm Professor Limoni," said the woman, holding out her hand. Antonio stood up and shook the professor's hand while Maria just watched.

"It's our square, too," she muttered darkly, flicking her eyes over Professor Limoni.

"Of course it is," replied the professor. "Do you mind if we share it for a few minutes? I'm meeting Professor Roberts for a coffee. Can I wait here?" She pointed at a nearby table.

"OK," said Maria, who had never been asked permission for anything before. She thought she had better say something else.

"Do you want a shot?" she asked, holding out a marble.

"Thanks, but I don't know how to play," smiled the professor.

"But I do," came another voice. Antonio and Maria looked up to see the American man striding towards them.

"I'm the marble champ of the mid-west!" said Professor Roberts, beaming. "Mind if I have a go?"

Maria nodded and smiled weakly. She held out
a handful of marbles, and the American professor
carefully selected his taw. He crouched down, and
with a practiced flick, knocked another marble out
of the circle.

"Your turn!" he said, challenging Maria.

She took careful aim, and whacked a marble straight into Antonio's favourite, lying just inside the circle. It cracked out, and rolled toward Professor Roberts.

Suddenly, Professor Roberts frowned. He turned his head to one side, and stared at Antonio's marble. Carefully, he reached down and picked it up.

"Hey, that's not allowed!" protested Maria.

"Sorry," smiled Professor Roberts. "Where did you get this?" he asked Antonio.

Antonio looked nervous. "I didn't steal it," he said. "I found it."

The American smiled and nodded.

"I'm sure you didn't steal it," he replied. "But I am interested, where did you find it?"

"Up there," said Antonio, waving in the direction of Mount Pyros.

"Where, up there?" asked Professor Roberts, with a serious voice.

"In *our* field," mumbled Antonio. "If it was on our field, that means it belongs to me," he added, feeling defensive.

Professor Roberts held up the marble and examined it closely, then passed it onto Professor Limoni.

"Is that what I think it is?" he asked quietly. After a few seconds, Professor Limoni nodded silently.

"Have you ever found anything else in your field?" she asked trying to stay calm. "White rocks, or pieces of metal?"

"Sure," replied Antonio. "Dad uses white rocks to mend the walls around the field all the time."

The two professors looked excitedly at each other. Antonio wondered what was going on. Maria stood up, with her hands on her hips.

"Can we have our marble back, please!" she demanded. "We're in the middle of a game here, you know."

Chapter 3

The Hunt For Treasure

Mayor Gruffio sat back in his chair behind an untidy desk, and mopped the sweat off his brow.

"After we saw the Roman marble, and heard about the white rocks, we just had to go and have a look at the farm," explained Professor Roberts excitedly.

"And when we got there, we found many fragments of polished stone, just like those carved for use in Roman buildings," added Professor Limoni.

"We believe there is enough evidence to investigate this site further. If the stories about the lost town of Polonium and the eruption of Mount Pyros two thousand years ago are true, there could be all sorts of archaeological treasures lying underneath that field."

At the word 'treasures', Gruffio sat up. His beady eyes looked from one professor to the other.

"Indeed," he wheezed eagerly. "But, of course, you will need *council* permission to start excavating." He waved his flabby hand over the papers that lay scattered across his desk. "There will be, naturally, a lot of paperwork. It might take weeks. And, of course we should find out how the farmer feels about it."

"Armenio doesn't mind," said Professor Roberts. "He says nothing grows in that field anyway. As long as we don't disturb his walls, he's happy for us to start digging."

"Really?" said Gruffio, with a hint of a frown. "Well, he shouldn't agree to things without the mayor's permission, of course."

Gruffio eased himself out of his chair and stood up.

"I understand you won't be back for a week or so," he said. "Until you get your team together, you can't start work."

"That's right," agreed Professor Limoni.

"Well, leave it with me," said Gruffio, with a sickly smile. "I'll make sure all the papers are completed and given to the council by the time you return."

As soon as the two archaeologists had left, Gruffio greedily placed his hands around his phone and dialled a number.

"Uncle Nostro," he whispered in an excited voice. "It's Gruffio. I think we are about to become rich. Very rich!" He grinned into the phone, and started laughing in an evil way.

* * * *

The next morning, Armenio was woken by a loud, thundering, rumbling noise. The floor of the house was shaking beneath him. Even the walls shook.

"Dad, what's going on?" called Antonio's frightened voice from the next room.

"Is it an earthquake?" asked Maria, peering anxiously around the door. "What is it?"

Armenio immediately leapt out of bed and flung open the curtains. When he saw what was happening outside, his mouth dropped open, and his eyes widened. A look of anger flashed across his face.

"What do they think they are doing?" he cried, quickly stuffing his feet into a pair of boots. Still wearing his pyjamas, he stormed outside.

"What is all this?" he yelled. Two giant bulldozers, with the words 'Nostro Earthmoving', were crawling towards his field, crushing grapevines in their path.

"Good morning, Armenio," grinned Mayor Gruffio. The walk up the path from Poloni had been more exertion than usual for the lazy mayor, and his forehead was dripping with sweat. Still he managed to hold out a large piece of paper.

Armenio grabbed the paper. "What does this mean, Gruffio?"

Gruffio smiled and folded his arms across his huge belly.

"Essential earthworks," he replied. "This is a council order, declaring that essential earthworks are needed. Right here, in fact." Gruffio waved at the bulldozers to continue.

Suddenly, Armenio realised what was going on. He stared furiously at Gruffio.

"It's what those professors found, isn't it? You want to find the treasure first, don't you?"

Gruffio tried to look shocked, as he shook his head. Tiny beads of sweat flew off.

"I wouldn't dream of such a selfish act," he said sounding hurt, but his greedy little eyes gave him away.

"Essential earthworks," he repeated, pointing at the paper. "All legal, and signed by ... the mayor, of course. There's nothing you can do!"

The bulldozers lowered their giant blades and started tearing huge strips of grass and soil away from the surface of Armenio's field. The roar of their engines drowned out the next few sentences that Armenio said to the mayor.

Armenio stomped angrily back to his house, where Antonio and Maria stood waiting.

"Quickly," he said. "Run down to the village and ask Mrs Rivoli if you can use her telephone. Call your friends, the professors, and tell them what's going on. We need to stop these madmen before they destroy everything."

The children raced out of the house.

Armenio ran back outside and headed to his field. He dashed between the bulldozers, and sat down, right in the middle of his land, with his arms firmly folded.

If the bulldozers were going to dig up his field, they would have to dig him up with it!

Chapter **4**

An Immortal Meeting

"Come now, Armenio," pleaded Mayor Gruffio.
"If you don't move, we shall have to move you."
He rattled the piece of paper in Armenio's face.
"Essential earthworks. Council order."

Armenio sat, stony-faced, staring at the giant blade
of a bulldozer, an arm's length from his face.

"OK," shrugged the mayor. "We warned you."
He waved at one of the bulldozer drivers, who
clambered back up into the driver's seat. If
Armenio wouldn't move, they would have to
bulldoze him out of the way.

Suddenly, just as the driver reached for the key to start the machine, an earth-shattering boom split the air. The field buckled and shook, as if it were a piece of carpet being shaken out. Gruffio grabbed hold of one of the bulldozers to steady himself.

"What ... what was that?" he cried.

There was another terrifying growl, and the earth shook again. Even Armenio stood up.

What he saw next shocked him even more than the presence of bulldozers on his field.

"Look!" he gasped. "The mountain!"

A small wisp of smoke rose from the craggy peak of Mount Pyros. The mountain shook again and, as if to confirm what was going on, another burst of smoke poured out from the peak.

Moments later, there was a violent earthquake. As the bulldozers shook and swayed in the soil, their drivers leapt off, and ran down the pathway, screaming with fright.

"Come back!" wailed Gruffio. "It's only a bit of a shake and some smoke!"

The ground lurched again, and one of the bulldozers started to sink even further into the ground. Somewhere, far beneath the surface, there was a groaning, rumbling sound.

Armenio leapt back, just in time, but Gruffio hadn't realised what was happening until too late. The heavy bulldozer slipped over onto its side and an enormous hole appeared in the earth beneath its tracks.

Like an avalanche, the soil rolled over into the hole, the weight of the bulldozer dragging it down until it too disappeared beneath the surface of the field.

Everything was happening so fast that, when Armenio turned, he saw a pair of flabby hands, scrambling at tufts of grass just before they, too, slipped into the gaping hole. Gruffio, an entire bulldozer, and half of Armenio's field, had disappeared.

The professors arrived three hours later, escorted
by the wailing sounds of a police car and several
other vehicles full of important-looking people.
But by that time, Mount Pyros had settled and,
as they drove up the path to the farm, they were
astonished to witness such an unbelievable scene.

Armenio, Antonio and Maria were sitting in the middle of their field, at the edge of what looked like a deep crater. Another bulldozer lay at a crazy angle, halfway down another smaller hole in the ground.

Armenio and the children stood up and waved at the procession of cars weaving their way towards their field.

Finally, everyone gathered around the edge of the deepest, darkest hole.

"There must be a large building underneath," said Professor Roberts, peering down into the hole. "The eruption has collapsed the roof, exposing a hole."

"A building?" asked Armenio incredulously.

Professor Limoni nodded. "In an eruption like the one we think happened here two thousand

years ago, it wouldn't be unusual for whole
buildings to be covered with many metres of mud
and ash, and for people in these buildings to have
been buried alive! All your soil has come from the
mountain — and it has covered up everything that
was once here."

A faint voice came from deep inside the hole.

"Help!"

Armenio grinned wickedly. "Gruffio," he said, nodding towards the hole. "Unfortunately, the bulldozer didn't squash him. But he can't climb out. The soil just falls in on top of him whenever he tries to get out."

"Get me out!" came the faint voice. "Please, there's a ... a *thing* down here!"

"What sort of thing?" called out Professor Limoni.

"It looks like a ... person," came the shaky reply.

"Hand me that torch," said Professor Roberts, beckoning to a policeman. He carefully crept to the edge of the cavern, shone the beam down into the darkness and whistled.

"Wow!" he said. "Even with the wreckage of a bulldozer on top of it, this looks impressive."

"What can you see?" asked Maria.

"It's a room alright," said the professor. "A huge, expensively decorated room, by the looks of it. Perfectly preserved. Wait! What's that? There's something carved on one of the walls, above a doorway."

The professor slowly spelled out a word.

"G-R-U-S-I-U-S. Grusius!" He stared at Professor Limoni. "The mad governor of Polonium! I think we've found his palace."

"Get me out of here! This ... this *thing* is scaring me!"

The professor swung his torch beam in the direction of Gruffio's pleading voice, to find Gruffio's eyes, wide with terror, staring up at him. And then he spotted something else.

It seemed like a jumbled mound of purple material. Around it lay the remains of some broken glass, and the outline of a dark stain on the mosaic floor. With a sudden shock, Professor Roberts realised what — or rather, who — he was looking at.

"Congratulations," he whispered down to Gruffio, who looked as if he was about to cry.

"What do you mean?" blubbered back the mayor.

"You're going to be famous," grinned Professor Roberts. "Your name will be remembered forever — as the name of the man who, after two thousand years, first laid his eyes on the perfectly preserved body of the immortal Grusius!"

There was silence around the hole, as everyone realised the importance of this amazing discovery — a perfectly preserved but very dead Roman, in a perfectly preserved Roman palace.

And then the silence was broken, by a long, mournful wail. A wail that seemed to echo through century upon century.

"Get me out of here ... now!"